Beale's Hawk Down

a Night Stalker story
by
M. L. Buchman

Buchman Bookworks

Other works by M.L. Buchman

The Night Stalkers

The Night Is Mine
I Own the Dawn
Daniel's Christmas
Wait Until Dark
Frank's Independence Day
Peter's Christmas
Take Over at Midnight
Light Up the Night
Bring On the Dusk

Firehawks

Pure Heat
Wildfire at Dawn
Full Blaze
Wildfire at Larch Creek

Angelo's Hearth

Where Dreams are Born
Where Dreams Reside
Maria's Christmas Table
Where Dreams Unfold
Where Dreams Are Written

Dieties Anonymous
Cookbook from Hell: Reheated
Saviors 101

Thrillers
Swap Out!
One Chef!
Two Chef!

SF/F Titles
Nara
Monk's Maze

Seven Years Ago

1

The Black Hawk helicopter shredded around her. The spin and fall fast enough that only the harness kept her in her seat.

The star-cracked glass-laminate windshield—each star centered around the hole where an armor-piercing round had punched into the cockpit—fragmented Lieutenant Emily Beale's view of the outside world into a thousand tiny refracted images. The veering Thai jungle hacked into crystalline shards of green in a thousand hues.

Hydraulic fluid sprayed over the outside of the windshield. Altered the colors of the world around them to a dark, alien-realm red. Even the yellow sunlight bled vermillion.

Emily flicked off the primary hydraulic system. The secondary didn't take over, but the emergency backup hung on.

"Beale!" Larry shouted at her from the pilot's seat. "I can't see!"

Emily glanced over and saw blood dribbling down over his forehead. One of the rounds had punched him high in the helmet, hopefully just a scalp wound.

She stopped attempting to recover systems and clamped her hands onto the controls. They were heavy, sluggish. The intercom sounded dead, Larry's shout had traveled across the cockpit, not into the headphones built into her helmet.

She clicked the mic switch a few times—with no result.

There wasn't time to look down, but the acrid stench of scorched electronics told her what had happened to their radios.

"Can't see much myself," she shouted back.

Emily watched out the only clear section of her copilot's side window, an intact area little bigger than her hand. She had to wait only two seconds for the helicopter to spin through a full three-sixty and reveal her options of where to crash.

South and east, a broad spread of poppy fields. They'd been flying east to west when they stumbled on the fields and been fired upon immediately. Even shot up, they'd managed to overfly most of the fields. She spotted several vehicles racing across it in their direction, they'd be in range in three minutes; up close and personal within five. The rugged terrain of the foothills to the Luang Prabang Range was in her favor, or would be until the Black Hawk hit the rolling fields.

"Poppies!" the Wicked Witch of the West seemed to cackle in her ears. They hadn't known about the poppy fields. Their flight had been racing northwest on a flood-relief mission. But some Thai opium lord hadn't liked the pair of U.S. Army helicopters flying low over his fields.

North and west was helicopter-killing jungle. Though by the vibrations building up in the controls and the airframe, there wasn't much left to kill except the pilot and copilot. The crew chiefs? The silence of the two big M240 machine guns that they should be using to hammer back at the people who had just shot up the helicopter were ominously silent.

The second spin around let her spot the burning wreckage of their sister helicopter. The 101st Airborne Screaming Eagles were gonna be some kind of pissed. She just had to stay alive long enough for that to matter.

Emily risked taking one hand off the controls to trigger her personal radio tucked in her vest pocket. "Mayday! Mayday! Mayday! Army flight—" Larry lost control of their flight angle and she had to retake the controls and simply pray that someone had heard her. The rising screams of the dying Black Hawk masked any response. If there was one.

"I'm taking us into the trees, Larry."

"That sounds like fun."

It was too much effort to shout over the roar of the rotors and all of the systems alarms blaring for attention. She concentrated on landing without killing them.

On the next spin, she initiated a roll. Larry leaned his support into the rapidly failing controls and she was glad for every ounce of help.

By tipping the wounded Black Hawk well onto its side, she managed to counter the spin that the rudder pedals could no longer wholly fix. But it also meant she was losing altitude—at little better than a plummet.

There was now as much red inside in cockpit as outside. What electronics were still with them were blinking red warnings. Alarms were blaring but she didn't have time or the free hand to silence them.

Larry took a hand off the collective to kill the worst of them. But it was clear by how his hand fumbled slightly that he still couldn't see and was doing it based solely on training.

They were going down no matter what.

No time like the present.

If they hung up in a tree, they'd be shot before they could climb down.

If they hit the jungle floor directly, they'd just be dead.

Emily aimed ten tons of dying Black Hawk helicopter into the crown of a fig tree, hoping it would break their fall, but she wanted to hit it off center enough for them to slide down to the forest floor.

That all sounded great…if she'd had any control.

She didn't.

One last try on the radios. Nothing.

"Brace yourself," a shout to Larry.

The Black Hawk finally rolled onto its side as they hit the trees.

Rotor blades hacked at foliage, hit branches, crumpled, and broke away. The twin turboshaft engines, no longer trying to turn the long rotor blades, raced wildly out of control. She managed one T-handle engine cut off and Larry managed the other as the body of the helicopter slammed into the fig tree she'd targeted and tumbled off into an oak on the way to its doom.

2

Only after they hit was Emily able to reconstruct where "up" was and that by some miracle they'd landed tail first. The rear of the helicopter had acted as a giant shock absorber as it crushed.

Then they flopped forward onto the wheels. The shock absorbers managed to bounce and they were parked right side up on the jungle floor. The helo was tipped back and thirty degrees to her side, but they were down.

A massive root system, which wound and snarled like a thousand giant snakes,

was pressed against Larry's door. She
tried to shove her door open. It opened
six inches then caught on the jungle floor.
Throwing her shoulder into it gained her
only another three inches.

Emily popped her harness, managed
to contort her long legs up to the main
windscreen and kicked with both boots.
The shot-up laminate disintegrated into a
shower of a thousand crystalline shards.

Beyond the shattered remains of their
twenty million-dollar hi-tech cocoon lay
such a different world that it felt as if she
was in some science fiction movie looking
through a rip in the space-time continuum.

All around her the dead helicopter
still blinked and wept. She powered down
the few surviving systems and the last
of the alarms descended into silence, but
still-creaking metal and the steady drip of
leaking fluids surrounded her.

Mere feet away stood a shadowed jungle
unlike anything she'd ever seen. No training
in the swamps of Mississippi had given
her a calibration for what she was seeing.
Tree trunks a dozen feet across and fifty

to a hundred feet high soared above them. The undergrowth was thick with leaves that were as big as she was and seemed as big as her helicopter. The silence of it was breathless. And the smell was—the tang of blood, the bite of hydraulic fluid, and the nasty, sharp, warning stench of kerosene-laden fuel.

Larry was struggling with his door, unaware of the massive tree-trunk blocking his way.

Survive!

The shouted self instruction finally shifted Emily into action.

"We're going out the windshield on my side."

Larry popped his harness and clumsily followed her out of the helo.

Once they were out, she leaned back in for her rifle. It wasn't in the door's mount anymore. Nor was Larry's.

She'd flown beside the Night Stalkers of the Army's 160th Special Operations Aviation Regiment a few times and now understood why they always wore their weapons across the front of their vests even in training flights. It was a practice she would certainly adopt. If she survived this.

Emily circled around to the crew chief's gun window on her side of the helo. The open-eyed bloody face that confronted her was identifiable only by which side of the aircraft it was on.

Down here beneath the forest's canopy, midday was dusk and the Black Hawk's interior was midnight. She fished a flashlight out of her thigh pouch and shone it over Vincenzo's head. Yamota was no better off. Her attempts to wrench open the helo's side door were futile, it was trapped by the badly twisted frame.

She considered dismounting Vincenzo's M240, and then she looked again at the waiting jungle. It was going to be challenge enough without a twenty-seven pound machine gun and the same weight again in ammunition. Her and Larry's best chances were in evasion, not confrontation.

Bracing herself emotionally, she tipped Vincenzo back far enough that she could strip him of his holstered sidearm and spare magazines. He had a pair of full water bottles tucked into pockets as well. She took those despite the slickness of blood on plastic. Pretending that it was only red water spilled over the outsides didn't help in the least.

Larry was no longer standing at the nose of the helo when she returned. Instead he'd slid down to the jungle mulch and was leaning against the rounded nose cone, the only undamaged panel of the entire aircraft.

He had wiped his face of the worst of the blood and was blinking normally. But when she waved a hand in front of his eyes, he didn't react. She leaned back into the helicopter and managed to find her med-kit, which she stuffed into a vest pocket. Another future lesson to keep everything she'd ever need on her person.

It was all very well back in the classroom to believe that you'd have the on-going resources of your downed helicopter and that the instructors had just been blowing their usual smoke. Besides, for every hour of survival training there was a hundred hours of flight training and a hundred more of combat training. That made it easy to discount the one hour that was squeezed in here and there. During Iraq and Afghanistan they didn't even have time for that.

After a moment's debate, Emily removed her helmet. She wanted its protection, but needed her ears uncovered. The instant she did so, the world came crashing in. Bird calls came bursting to life around her, all commenting on the helicopter that had just plummeted into their midst. And it wasn't the comfortable *check check* of a red-wing blackbird or a crow's sharp *caw.* The jungle chittered and nattered and the occasional spine-tingled *scree!* sliced through the air.

Also, now that she'd shed her helmet, she could hear the racing engines of pickup trucks as they roared across the poppy fields in their direction. As well as Emily could judge, she and Larry still had a few minutes, but "few" was the operative word.

She considered removing Larry's helmet, but didn't think she'd like what she found there. Besides, his blindness— whether temporary or permanent—meant he needed protection to not batter his face against branches as they forged into the undergrowth.

There was no question that's where they were going. To stay by the helicopter would only guarantee their doom.

"C'mon, Larry. Let's get a move on." He stumbled uncertainly to his feet when she pulled on his arm.

"What about Vincenzo and Yamota?"

"We need to get going if we don't want to join them."

"Shit." Not even emphatic enough to earn an exclamation point. The four of them had flown two tours in Iraq and Afghanistan. There was no way to encapsulate or deal with such a loss in this moment. Focus on the next task. Survive.

Their Black Hawk had a transport configuration, but it wasn't all about moving howitzers and supplies. They'd flown hundreds of infantry delivery and retrieval missions, combat search and rescue, and pretty much everything under the sun that wasn't covered by the Special Operations guys of the Night Stalkers. They'd even flown a few special ops missions when SOAR was strapped for resources in a particular region.

To survive all of that and then lose two men on a flood-relief flight halfway around the world was too painful to elicit external emotion, the internal anguish was far too great.

As was the need to survive.

Emily pulled Larry's arm over her shoulder and locked her arm around his waist. It would be easier to guide his steps that way.

She stared at the thick undergrowth and wished for a machete. Then she thought better of it. That would just make them that much easier to track.

With that in mind, she tossed her helmet toward the far side of the clearing punched by the Black Hawk's crash. It landed against the edge of a small gap in the branches. Maybe the bad guys would think they'd gone that direction, deeper into the jungle.

Deeper into the jungle. That's exactly what they'd expect.

Never do the expected, some drill Sergeant's voice echoed out of her past. McCluskey?

"I'd pay good money right now to have taken SERE." The Survival, Evasion, Resistance, and Escape course was mainly for Special Operations guys.

"Probably be real handy at the moment," Larry agreed. "When it really hits the wall, Emily, you leave me and take off."

"Don't be an idiot."

"Exactly. Don't be an idiot. If they're going to catch one of us or both of us, make it only one."

Emily kept her mouth shut. There was no chance in hell she was going to be leaving a live man behind.

"So, where are we going?"

"Back to the poppy fields," she checked the compass on her wrist. Who ever thought that a helicopter pilot would have need of a simple, mechanical compass. But the sun was straight overhead, she could barely see even that much through the thick canopy of branches and leaves, and it offered no indication of east or west.

"We're doing *what?*"

"You need to keep your voice down."

The approaching roar of the truck engines reinforced her. They'd been in the clearing under a minute. It had already been too long.

She led them around the tree that was pressed hard against Larry's door, and ducked under a massive leaf that dripped with the thick moisture despite the heat. Away from the helo her nose was assaulted with the foreignness of the jungle. Life so thick that she couldn't sort flower from fruit from rotting debris that rustled beneath their boots but also hid their footprints.

Because their arms were wrapped around each other, Larry had little choice but to follow.

They disappeared into the shadowy foliage.

3

Captain Larry Engstrom stumbled in a haze of red and gray shadows. He'd wiped his eyes clear of the blood, but it had made no difference. While Emily had scouted, he'd tried covering and uncovering his eyes to no effect. The play of light was from his optic nerves, not from his eyes.

He'd started to remove his helmet, but the slicing pain had added stars to the red and gray shadows. It had also taken his legs out from under him, dropping him to the jungle floor until Emily had hauled him back to his feet. His body screamed in a dozen places, but he was alive and that was all that mattered.

His father had begged him to get out. Begged him to do anything else, even something non-practical like music. His mother had simply looked sad and suddenly old. They had grown up protesting the Vietnam War. He had grown up in a different world where the United States was no longer the invader but now the invaded. The twin towers of the World Trade Center had gone down on his sixteenth birthday. He was twenty-two when he graduated from West Point and both Iraq and the Afghanistan Wars were in their fourth-year of constant escalation. His country had called and he'd answered.

A branch clunked hard against his helmet and sent him staggering into Emily.

He heard a whispered, "Sorry," over the ringing in his ears.

"Just stung for a moment," his head was still ringing but he didn't want to upset Emily. His beautiful Emily. He'd follow her to the ends of the Earth, if he could only make his feet work.

Larry had been stumbling along through his career much as he was now stumbling along the Thai jungle floor. Bravado, broads, and beer—the three "B"s of the Army. He took stupid risks and buried them in alcohol and his dick in willing women…until Second Lieutenant Emily Beale had boarded his Black Hawk.

A tall, slender blond who should have been on a fashion runway, not a militarized mess like Bagram. At first he'd convinced himself that she was a heat mirage or a magical genie, like *I Dream of Jeannie* sprung to life. Barbara Eden had been hot back in her day, but Emily Beale, a soldier with a steel spine and the integrity to match, totally dusted her.

He'd cleaned up his act to meet her standard. And once he had, he couldn't believe the shit he'd done in the past or his low-life taste in women. Beale had kept their relationship strictly professional— right through two tours and her promotion to First Lieutenant and his to Captain—but at least on the few occasions he went womanizing, he'd shown a much better taste in women and been more respectful. With the Emily Beale gold-standard for comparison, it wasn't hard.

She was hurrying them along and he did his best to keep his breathing quiet though it sounded loud and ragged despite the insulation of his helmet.

Lately things had been shifting between them. Over the last year they'd grown closer. She'd let her hair down a few times and they'd talked over a beer and pizza about their careers and a little about their lives before.

Their lives before...

With a loud *tonk* that seemed to echo through the jungle, Larry caught his boot on a tree root and had to wrap both hands around Emily to keep his balance. She felt so good that it was hard to let go of her. He could feel her determination when he felt so little of it remaining. He knew he was injured and only adrenaline was keeping him upright, adrenaline and, again, the need to meet her standard.

Their lives before oddly no longer mattered. Her dad was some government bigwig, though she declined to say which one. His was a game-software engineer. Her mom: socialite. His: grade school teacher. It didn't matter. They were soldiers now and moving up through the ranks of the 101st Airborne.

The racing truck engines were close now. Even the jungle didn't muffle them.

Then brakes squealed, tires skidded on gravel. A raking slash of machine-gun fire sent bullets whistling through the leaves overhead. Birds screamed in surprise and departed in noisy flocks.

Emily was pulling on his arm, dragging him to the side, ducking for cover.

He didn't need the urgency transmitted through her guiding arm, still locked around his waist, to know they only had seconds to find cover. He'd scream in frustration if he dared. Blind. Unable to help. Deadweight.

4

Emily blessed every time Larry managed to place one foot in front of the other; he was far too big for her to carry.

He'd been beer-belly bound when she first met him, as wild as most of the pilots in the 101st. Dangerous as hell and on the road down. At least she'd thought he was. Then he'd begun working out more, drinking less, and was soon as fit as he was handsome. He'd also been an exceptional flyer; she'd learned a great deal from Larry Engstrom.

And now he was proving himself to be far above the standard soldier with how he was fighting against the pain and blindness, helping as much as he could.

The pointless gun fire slicing over their heads continued killing leaves.

By the sounds from the vehicles, she'd made a crucial mistake. She'd headed straight from the helicopter back toward the poppy fields. Of course, that was exactly the route the bad guys would take from their vehicles to look for the helo. Should've arced.

Stupid!

It didn't matter that she was a city girl from Washington D.C., she wasn't allowed stupid. Not when the slightest mistake was going to kill them.

Taking advantage of the masking noise of the gunfire, she twisted due north to get out of their direct line of approach toward the crash site.

The gunfire sliced off as if cut with a knife. The sudden silence of the jungle thundered down on them and she froze in place. There wasn't a single bird call. Not even a rustle of something moving through the undergrowth.

Then the shouts in Thai began—so close to hand she almost answered their calls to each other.

Under cover of their shouts, she dragged Larry sideways into a particularly dense clump of undergrowth. Banana, papaya, or Dr. Suess Truffula trees—she hadn't a clue.

Dragging him down to the jungle floor didn't take much effort. The adrenaline of the crash and their race through the trees could only last so long and it was collapsing out from under her.

She landed hard, but stifled her grunt. Larry fell too, mostly on top of her.

He started to move, but she held him close as a pair of feet and many curses crashed through the brush not a half dozen paces away.

5

Larry tried to do the decent thing, but he was so tired. He couldn't hear much of anything through the helmet. Someone shouted from a distance away, but he had no way to tell how far. Or how angry.

But while he could neither see nor hear, he could absolutely feel. Despite service revolvers, flight vests, and circumstances— against all odds he was finally holding Emily Beale tightly in his grasp and he was loathe to let go.

Even with all the gear they wore, he could feel how they would be in each other's arms.

He was past fear now. And, he realized, far past any shred of common sense. It was easy to pretend for a moment that they were on some tropical island—preferably one where no one was trying to kill them—and they could drift together. Turquoise water.

First signs of shock from blood loss, some distant part of him noted. Which was odd, there was no more blood running down his face from the scalp wound, but he was past caring about that.

Larry's nose was still working just fine. He could smell the dark richness of the decaying plant matter that made up the jungle floor—a thick, soft mattress of duff. And also the scent of Emily Beale that he'd know among a thousand flowers: rare, elusive, enticing.

"Don't move," her whisper was just loud enough to penetrate his helmet, but no more.

"Be still my heart," he whispered against her neck and cursed the helmet he wore that let him get no closer.

But her vest had ridden upward off her waist when they'd tumbled to the ground.

His hands slid up past her sidearm and wrapped around her waist. Again he imagined what it would feel like to make love to Emily Beale as he had done through a thousand cold showers.

Not some hurried, frantic tumble like with most women found in soldier bars. It was as if they were seeking desperately to cling onto a life, any life, because they didn't have one of their own. Emily wasn't like that. Emily *was* life. She was perhaps the most alive person Larry had ever known.

To make love to her wouldn't be a matter of minutes, hours, or even days. It was a task that could stretch out as a constant discovery over years.

Larry had never thought about years before when it came to women, but the one in his arms now made it seem totally natural.

He snuggled against Emily the best he could, and breathed her life in.

6

Emily wasn't surprised when Larry clung so tightly to her. His feelings for her had been clear from the moment she'd deplaned into the mayhem of Bagram Airfield.

Her efforts to keep him at a distance had slowly weakened. Once he stopped drinking so much, she began to know the immensely skilled flyer. And once he got over the macho, testosterone-poisoned standards that were clearly a pre-req for applying to the 101st Combat Aviation Brigade, she had discovered that Larry

Engstrom was a thoroughly decent man. A discovery that seemed to surprise him as much as it did her.

Captain Engstrom was an easy man to respect, but Larry had become a friend. And despite the dangers of fraternization within the U.S. military, she'd begun leaning toward finding a common vacation spot for their next leave. Hawaii always sounded like the right place for something like that.

Also, letting him cling to her served to keep him quiet.

She knew it wasn't his fault, because he was blind, but he'd stumbled over every single obstacle like a bull in a china shop no matter how carefully she'd guided him.

There were more shouts. They'd reached the helo which couldn't be more than a few hundred meters away; she and Larry had not been moving quickly.

They bought the ruse. The sounds of the pack of Thai bandits went hying off into the distance like a pack of rabid hounds—music to her ears.

She kept listening, ignoring how it felt to have Larry's hands tight about her waist.

It felt good—too long since she'd been held close by a man.

Then he shifted and kissed her.

It wasn't some intense or passionate kiss as she'd imagined. Neither was it testing and teasing. It was nice, but it was as if Larry wasn't really all there for it.

A harsh rattle of the powerful M240 broke them apart. Someone had climbed aboard the downed helo and was having fun with the weapon.

There were numerous shouts and curses.

Larry didn't try to reengage, not that she'd encourage it under their present circumstances. But while she listened for any approaches that circled too close to their hideout, his condition began to worry her.

While they'd been on the move, he'd done well enough. But his hands were no longer holding her as tightly.

7

Larry felt as if he was floating when someone...Emily, rolled him onto his back.

It felt so good to lie here beside her.

If only it wasn't so cold.

"When did the Thai jungle get so cold?" He fought against a shiver.

There was a distant zing of pain as someone...Emily? Yamota?...pulled off his helmet.

He was glad to be rid of the weight.

Also, with the removal of the helmet, the pinch of pressure that had been giving him a splitting headache eased off. With

a spinning flash of color, so sharp that
it gave him a moment of vertigo, vision
returned to his left eye.

And the view was lovely.

Emily's elegant features, framed by her
straight, white-gold hair, hung just inches
above him.

"Hi, babe."

"Shh, Larry. You have to stay quiet."

"Right. Bad guys." Oops, he'd been
speaking aloud. "With guns." Shit! Shh.

So, he occupied himself with lying still
as Emily inspected him.

"Cold," he whispered.

He could see the worry on her face. He
didn't like seeing that. So instead he focused
on her neck. And imagined the rise of
breast he would encounter if he were to
start a hand there and slide it inside her
flightsuit. Any number of hot, sweaty
training sessions done in t-shirts had left
little enough to the imagination. So, he
preoccupied himself with imagining that
last bit.

Emily-of-the-perfect-breasts moved out
of his view. He felt her fingers poking and

prodding him with what he recognized as a medical assessment.

Her sharp hiss drew his attention back from imaging his mouth tracing down that neckline toward heaven.

"Shh," he reminded her. "Bad guys. With guns."

8

Emily opened the medical kit that she
knew was useless and looked in it anyway.

With five tons of medical supplies in
the back of the helo, none of them had
thought about loading up full combat
med kits. The kit she'd recovered from the
pocket of her copilot's door didn't have
thread and needle to attempt to put Larry
back together, even if she'd known how.
The small tube of skin glue wasn't going to
make much difference either.

The pantleg of his flightsuit was soaked
in blood. It wasn't arterial, but under the

circumstances that might have been a mercy. If the shot that caught him had cut an artery, he'd have bled out in a few minutes. Instead a line of bullets had passed through his thigh. Through-and-through meat shots and he'd been bleeding out of them the whole time.

She could stop those...maybe. He'd be weak and shocky from blood loss, but she could glue and bind him up in time if she hurried.

It wasn't only lack of vision that had him stumbling so badly. The adrenal miracle was that he'd walked on that leg at all.

Then she'd spotted more blood up at the webbed belt that his knife and holster hung from. Just a small blotch of it. A bullet had ricocheted off his sidearm, slipped in beneath the edge of the belt, then been covered and held closed when they'd climbed out of the helo and the belt had settled downward over the hole. The hole wasn't the problem.

Using his knife, she sliced open the flight suit to expose his belly. The tumbling bullet had torn up his internal organs.

His stomach was dark and distended with massive internal bleeding.

Larry was already dead.

9

Larry tried to pull Emily back into his arms.

She resisted for a moment and then lay down beside him.

"My beautiful Emily," he remembered there was some reason to whisper, he just couldn't quite recall why. He brushed a hand—so heavy to lift it—over her cheek and she struggled to smile for him. He could see it was hard.

Had he been too forward?

Then she took his hand in hers and pressed its palm against her cheek. His fingers left a blood-red imprint on her perfect skin.

"Are you bleeding?" he struggled to get up and check her for injuries.

"No, Larry. You are." Her whisper close beside his ear was the gentlest caress. He'd always imagined it would be like this with her. Then he made sense of her words.

"Me?" He saw the flash of pain inside those ice-blue eyes it had taken him so long to learn how to read. "That's alright then. As long as it isn't you."

"I'm okay."

"You're better than okay. You're my idea of a perfect wom—"

10

Emily clamped her hand over Larry's mouth.

The stealthy footstep sounded along the pathway she and Larry had battered through the undergrowth as she led them back toward the poppy fields.

She held her breath as she watched the entrance to their tiny bower. She didn't dare even reach for a gun or knife, because she didn't dare uncover Larry's mouth.

His lips were moving against her palm, way past knowing he shouldn't speak. Thankfully his muffled vocalizations were very weak. Too soft to understand even though she lay close against him.

The steps neared.

Larry, finally understanding that he shouldn't speak, looked up at her with his one good eye. The other eye tried to look up too, but kept drifting aside.

The steps moved past them as Larry's one good eye struggled to convey some message. But the drug lord's soldier had stopped to listen, or light a cigarette, or scratch himself.

There was a splashing sound.

He was taking a piss not three meters away. In moments she could smell it on the air.

Larry stared at her with his one eye as if trying to memorize her face.

Emily studied his face, knowing it was his last message, but she couldn't read it. Couldn't find what was important enough to be his last words.

Then he moved his lips one last time against her palm. He formed a kiss, closed his eyes, and died with a final sigh the same moment the soldier finished his business and moved farther off through the brush.

11

Emily never cried, it wasn't in her. But her eyes burned for a long time as Larry's hand cooled in hers through the afternoon and evening. The rescue force arrived in the darkness.

She never heard the helos that must have delivered the Combat Search-and-Rescue team. A group of the drug lord's men had camped at the jungle's edge, close enough that she could see their campfire's light through the trees and hear their soft talk.

Then there had been a series of soft spitting sounds, each accompanied by the distinctive click of a bolt returning on a silenced weapon. She listened, but couldn't hear any more Thai voices from the campfire.

She slowly, silently as possible, pulled the small velcroed patches aside that would reveal infrared-reflective patches. They would glow brightly if the person was wearing night-vision gear, identifying her as a "friendly."

Emily never heard the soldier approach. One moment she'd been alone with Larry's cold corpse and a moment later she knew she wasn't.

"First Lieutenant Emily Beale," she read off her service number to the silent darkness in a whisper.

"SEAL Commander Luke Altman, Lt. Beale. Pleasure to find you among the living."

"The only one."

His answer was a grim silence.

"The downed helo is another two hundred meters just south of west."

He transmitted the information to some of his colleagues.

Emily was at a loss as to how to move Larry when a rifle was pushed into her hands.

A moment later Larry's body was gone from beside her. With a grunt the SEAL shouldered Larry in a fireman's carry and then reached to take back his rifle. "Hang onto my belt and I'll lead you out of here, ma'am."

Emily walked into the darkness, trusting to the man to lead her just as Larry had trusted her. One hand on the SEAL's belt, the other once again holding Larry's chill hand—frozen with lifelessness despite the heat of the still, jungle night.

When she had considered being with Larry, she'd been forced to contemplate the possibility of losing the right to serve in the military. This morning, before his death, there had been a choice.

There wasn't any longer.

With simple gestures, a sudden rise of hip or a sideways shift, the SEAL led her around and over obstacles in the jungle. Having led Larry over the jungle floor, she could appreciate how effortlessly the SEAL guided her.

She had done all she could to save Larry. The man…it was hard to even think it…the man whose last message on Earth had been one of love. Love, like tears, wasn't in her, but the ache in her chest ran deep.

When they emerged beneath the starlight, she knew what she was going to do with the rest of her life.

It wasn't to pay back a debt. Nor revenge. It was a thankfulness. A thankfulness for Larry's love, for the SEAL's effortless guidance, for being alive. If she could one day be the person to stand outside a jungle bower and find not one living soldier, but two, it would be worth it.

When the black helicopters of the 160th SOAR descended through the night sky she let go of Larry's hand and thanked him silently.

Prior to this day, Emily had not known what she wanted to do next with her life. A West Pointer. An officer of the U.S. Army. A helicopter pilot for the 101st Screaming Eagles. She now understood that had been merely her preparation.

As she climbed aboard the Night Stalkers Black Hawk helicopter, she knew exactly what she was going to do next, even if the 160th SOAR didn't accept women.

When the pilot introduced himself over the intercom as Captain Mark Henderson, she considered informing him of who she was and that she would be flying beside him in a few years—female or not.

But she would let that wait. She'd let her actions speak rather than her words, for Larry had taught her how full and how much more important silence could be.

For now, she had faced death for the first time.

Emily was going to prove that it had not found her wanting.

About the Author

M. L. Buchman has over 30 novels in print. His military romantic suspense books have been named Barnes & Noble and NPR "Top 5 of the Year" and Booklist "Top 10 of the Year." In addition to romance, he also writes thrillers, fantasy, and science fiction.

In among his career as a corporate project manager he has: rebuilt and single-handed a fifty-foot sailboat, both flown and jumped out of airplanes, designed and built two houses, and bicycled solo around the world. He is now making his living as a full-time writer on the Oregon Coast with his beloved wife. He is constantly amazed at what you can do with a degree in Geophysics. You may keep up with his writing by subscribing to his newsletter at www.mlbuchman.com.

Target of Silence

-a new Night Stalkers team-
coming soon
(excerpt)

Major Pete Napier hovered his MH-60M
Black hawk helicopter ten kilometers
outside of Lhasa, Tibet and two inches off
the tundra. A mixed action team of Delta
Force and The Activity—the slipperiest
intel group on the planet—piled aboard
from both sides.

The rear cabin doors slid home with a
Thunk! Thunk! that sent a vibration through
his pilot's seat and an infinitesimal shift in
the cyclic control in his right hand. By the
time his crew chief could reach forward
to slap an "all secure" signal against his
shoulder, they were already fifty feet out
and ten up. That was enough altitude. He
kept the nose down as he clawed for speed
in the thin air at eleven thousand feet.

"Totally worth it," one of the D-boys
announced as soon as he was on the
intercom.

"Great, now I just need to get us out of
this alive."

"Do that, Pete. We'd appreciate it."

He wished to hell he had a stealth bird
like the one that had gone into bin Laden's
compound. But the one that had crashed
during that raid had been blown up. Where
there was one, there were always two, but
the second had gone back into hiding as
thoroughly as if it had never existed. He
hadn't heard a word about it since.

It was amazing, the largest city in Tibet
and ten kilometers away equaled barren

wilderness. He could crash out here and no one would know for decades unless some Yak herder stumbled upon them. Or was Yaks Mongolia? He was a dark-haired, corn-fed, white boy from Colorado, what did he know about Tibet? Most of the countries he'd flown into on black ops missions he'd only seen at night while moving very, very fast. Like now.

The inside of his visor was painted with overlapping readouts. A pre-defined terrain map, the best that modern satellite imaging could build made the first layer. This wasn't some crappy, on-line, look-at-a-picture-of-your-house display. Someone had a pile of dung outside their goat pen? He could see it, tell you how high it was, and probably say if they were pygmy goats or full-size LaManchas by the size of their shit-pellets.

On top of that readout was projected the forward-looking infrared camera images. The FLIR imaging gave him a real-time overlay, in case someone had put an addition onto their goat house since the last satellite pass, or parked their tractor across his intended flight path.

His nervous system was paying autonomic attention to that combined landscape. He was automatically compensating for the thin air at altitude as he instinctively chose when to start his climb over said goat house or his swerve around it.

It was the third layer, the tactical display that had most of his attention. To insert this deep into Tibet, without passing over Bhutan or Nepal, they'd had to add wingtanks on the helicopter's hardpoints where he'd much rather have a couple banks of Hellfire missiles.

At least he and the two Black Hawks which flew wingman on him were finally on the move.

While the action team was busy infiltrating the capital city and gathering intelligence on the particularly brutal Chinese assistant administrator, he and his crews had been squatting out in the wilderness under a large camouflage net designed to make his helo look like just another god-forsaken Himalayan lump of granite.

Command had determined that it was better to wait through the day than risk flying out and back in. He and his crew had stood shifts on guard duty, but none of them had slept. They'd been flying together too long to have any new jokes, so they'd played a lot of cribbage. He'd long ago ruled no gambling on deployment after a fistfight had broken out over a bluff that cost a Marine over three hundred dollars. Marines hated losing to Army. They'd had to sit on him for a long time before he calmed down.

Tonight's mission was part of an on-going campaign to discredit the Chinese "presence" in Tibet on the international stage—as if occupying the country the last sixty years didn't count toward ruling, whether invited or not. As usual, there was a crucial vote coming up at the U.N.—that, as usual, the Chinese could be guaranteed to ignore. However, the ever-hopeful CIA was in a hurry to make sure that any damaging information that they could validate was disseminated as thoroughly as possible prior to the vote.

Not his concern.

His concern was, were they going to pass over some Chinese sentry post at just under two hundred miles an hour? The sentries would then call down a couple Shenyang J-16 jet fighters that could hustle along at Mach 2 to fry his sorry ass. He knew there was a pair of them parked at Lhasa along with some older gear that would be just as effective against his three helos.

"Don't suppose you could get a move on, Pete?"

"Eat shit, Nicolai!" He was a good man to have as a copilot. Pete knew he was holding on too tight, and Nicolai knew that a joke was the right way to ease the moment.

He, Nicolai, and his fellow pilots had a long way to go tonight. They dove down into gorges and followed them as long as they dared. They hugged cliff walls at every opportunity to decrease their radar profile. And they climbed.

That was the true danger—they would be up near the Black Hawks' limits when they crossed over the backbone of the Himalayas in their rush for India. The air was so rarefied that they burned fuel at a prodigious rate. Their reserve didn't allow for any extended battles while crossing the border…not for any battle at all really.

# # #

It was pitch dark outside her helicopter when Captain Danielle Delacroix stamped on the left rudder pedal while giving the Black Hawk right control on cyclic. It tipped her most of the way onto her side, but let her continue in a straight line. A Black Hawk's rotor was fifty-four feet across. By cross-controlling her bird to tip it, she managed to execute a straight line between two pylons only thirty feet apart.

At her current angle of attack, she took up less than a half-rotor of width, twenty-four feet. That left her three feet to either side, sufficient as she was moving at under a hundred knots.

The training instructor sitting beside her in the copilot's seat didn't react as she swooped through the training course in Fort Campbell, Kentucky.

After two years of training with the U.S. Army's 160th Special Operations Aviation Regiment, she was ready for some action. At least she was convinced that she was. But the trainers of Fort Campbell, Kentucky had not signed off on her class yet. Nor had they given any hint of when they might.

She ducked under a bridge and bounced into a near vertical climb to clear the power line on the far side. Like a ride at *le carnaval,* only with five thousand horsepower.

To even apply to SOAR required five years of prior military rotorcraft experience. She had applied because of a chance encounter—or rather what she'd thought was a chance encounter at the time.

Captain Justin Roberts had been a top Chinook pilot, the one who had convinced her to cross-train from her beloved Black Hawk and try out the massive twin-rotor craft. He'd made the jump from the 10th Mountain Division to the 160th SOAR after he'd been in the service for five years.

Then one night she'd been having pizza in Watertown, New York a couple miles off the 10th's base at Fort Drum. Justin had greeted her with surprise and shared her pizza. Had said he was just in town visiting old haunts. Her questions had naturally led to discussions of his experiences at SOAR. He'd even paid for the pizza after eating half.

He'd left her interested enough to fill out an application to the 160th. The speed at which she was rushed into testing told her that her meeting with Justin hadn't been by chance and that she owed him more than half a pizza next time they met. She'd asked around, once she'd passed the qualification exams and a brutal set of interviews that had left her questioning her sanity, never mind her ability. "Justin Roberts is presently deployed, ma'am," was the only response she'd ever gotten.

The training course was never the same, but it always had a time limit. The time would be short and they didn't tell you what it was. So she drove the Black Hawk for all it was worth like Regina Jaquess waterskiing her way to U.S. Ski Team female athlete of the year.

The Night Stalkers were a damned secretive lot, and after two years of training, she understood why. With seven years flying for the 10th, she'd thought she was good.

She'd been one of the top pilots at Fort Drum.

The Night Stalkers had offered an education in what it really meant to fly. In the two years of training, she'd flown more hours than in the seven years prior, despite two deployments to Iraq. And spent more time in the classroom than her life-to-date accumulated flight hours.

But she was ready now. It was *très viscérale,* right down in her bones she could feel it. The Black Hawk was as much a part of her nervous system as breathing. As were the Little Bird and the massive Chinook.

She dove down into a canyon and slid to a hover mere inches over the reservoir inside the thirty-second window laid out on the flight plan.

Danielle resisted a sigh. She was ready for something to happen and to happen soon.

# # #

Pete Napier and his two fellow Black Hawks crossed into the mountainous province of Sikkim, India ten feet over the glaciers and still moving fast. It was an hour before dawn.

"Twenty minutes of fuel remaining," Nicolai said it like personal challenge when they hit the border.

"Thanks, I never would have noticed."

It had been a nail-biting tradeoff: the more fuel he burned, the more easily he climbed due to the lighter load. The more he climbed, the faster he burned what little fuel remained.

He climbed hard as Nicolai counted down the minutes remaining, burning fuel even faster than he had been crossing the mountains of southern Tibet. They caught up with the U.S. Air Force HC-130P Combat King refueling tanker with only ten minutes of fuel left.

"Ram that bitch."

Pete extended the refueling probe which extended beyond the forward edge of the rotor blade and drove at the basket trailing behind the tanker on its long hose.

He nailed it on the first try despite the fluky winds.

"Ah," Nicolai sighed. "It is better than the sex," his thick Russian accent only ever surfaced in this moment or in a bar while picking up women.

His helo had the least fuel due to having the most men aboard, so he was first in line. His Number Two picked up the second refueling basket trailing off the other wing of the HC-130P. A quick five hundred gallons and he was breathing much more easily.

Another two hours of—thank god— straight and level flight at altitude, and they arrived at the aircraft carrier awaiting them in the Bay of Bengal. India had agreed to turn a blind eye as long as the Americans never actually touched their soil.

Once out on deck—and the worst of the kinks worked out—he pulled his team together, six pilots and six crew chiefs.

"Honor to serve!" He saluted them sharply.

"Hell yeah!" They shouted in response and saluted in turn. It their version of spiking the football in the end zone.

A petty officer in a bright green vest appeared at his elbow, "Follow me please, sir." He pointed toward the Navy-gray command structure that towered above the carrier's deck. The Commodore of the entire carrier group was waiting for him just outside the entrance.

The green escorted him across the hazards of the busy flight deck. Pete pulled his helmet on to buffer the noise of an F-18 Hornet firing up and being flung off the catapult.

"Orders, Major Napier," the Commodore handed him a folded sheet. "Hate to lose you."

The Commodore saluted, which Pete automatically returned before looking down at the sheet of paper in his hands. The man was gone before the import of Pete's orders slammed in.

A different green showed up with his duffle and began guiding him toward a loading C-2 Greyhound twin prop airplane. It was parked number two for the launch catapult, close behind the raised jet-blast deflector.

What in the name of fuck-all had he done to deserve this?

He glanced at the orders again as he stumbled up the Greyhound's rear ramp and crash landed into a seat.

Training rookies?

It was worse than a demotion.

This was punishment.

***

Available at fine retailers everywhere

More information at:
www.mlbuchman.com

Other works by M.L. Buchman

The Night Stalkers

The Night Is Mine
I Own the Dawn
Daniel's Christmas
Wait Until Dark
Frank's Independence Day
Peter's Christmas
Take Over at Midnight
Light Up the Night
Bring On the Dusk

Firehawks

Pure Heat
Wildfire at Dawn
Full Blaze
Wildfire at Larch Creek

Angelo's Hearth

Where Dreams are Born
Where Dreams Reside
Maria's Christmas Table
Where Dreams Unfold
Where Dreams Are Written

Dieties Anonymous
Cookbook from Hell: Reheated
Saviors 101

Thrillers
Swap Out!
One Chef!
Two Chef!

SF/F Titles
Nara
Monk's Maze

CPSIA information can be obtained at www.ICGtesting.com
Printed in the USA
LVOW10s1622280515

440292LV00001B/12/P